LU, the Little LADYBUG and the GREAT WINTER

Idea and words by **Yuliya Barannikova**

Illustrations by Bohdana Bondar

For my Mother. With Love

This is the story of a little ladybug named Lu who loved to fly.

On sunny days, Lu loved to sit on her white daisy and soar through the sky together with the other ladybugs. She also liked to look at the clouds in the sky during the day and count the twinkling stars at night.

It never occurred to Lu that this might all change.

One day, Lu noticed that the trees around her looked different...

They were not green anymore; instead, they had turned yellow, orange, and red.

A couple of days later, they had even fewer leaves on them. Then, no leaves at all!

Whoosh! Whoosh!

Her lovely daisy began to wilt, too. The daisy's white petals fluttered down to the ground.

Lu decided to ask her friend the butterfly what was going on.

She found her carrying some leaves back to her home.

"Mrs. Butterfly, where have the warm and sunny days gone to?" cried Lu.

"Oh, don't you know? Winter is coming!" answered Mrs. Butterfly.

"Winter?" asked Lu with a puzzled look. "What's winter?"

But Mrs. Butterfly was too busy preparing her hole in the tree to answer Lu.

The little ladybug decided to ask her friends the ants. She found them carrying some food back to their ant house.

"Ants!" cried Lu. "Have you two ever heard of winter?"
"Oh yes, we have! It's the coldest time of the year!" they answered.

"We're saving food for the whole winter in case we decide to wake up from our deep sleep."

"Cold?" said Lu with a puzzled look. "What's cold?"
But the ants were too busy storing food to answer Lu.

Lu had never felt a cold day in her short ladybug life, so she didn't understand what winter was. She fluttered her wings and decided to ask Mrs. Spider.

"Mrs. Spider!" cried out the little ladybug, "Cold is coming! Who is this COLD?" she asked.

"Well, it's not WHO," said Mrs. Spider wrapping up her spider web.

"When it's cold, I won't be able to spin my webs anymore. I'll have to find some warm place to rest for a long time."

"Should I also look for a warm place?" asked Lu.

But the spider was too busy putting away her web to answer Lu.

Whoosh! Whoosh!

Soon Lu finally felt what cold was. Her little body couldn't stand it!

It was Lu's first time seeing white snow.

Lu felt lonely in this new world.

She started crying little ladybug tears...

Suddenly, Lu saw one of her ladybug friends flying towards her.

"Lu, where have you been?" asked the ladybug. "I have been looking everywhere for you. Winter is almost here!"

"I don't like winter! It's far too cold! I want summer to come back!" cried Lu.

At that very moment, they heard a soft voice from nearby.

It was an old stag beetle sitting on a branch.

"Oh, young lady, winter is not all that bad!" he said. "I felt the same way when I had my first winter."

"What do you mean? Have you experienced many winters?" asked the little ladybug, feeling confused.

"Why yes, I have! I've lived through many of them!" bubbled the old stag beetle. "We cannot stop the winter. It's a part of life!"

The two ladybugs crawled closer to the hollow, ready to hear more...

"You should take a rest and get ready to welcome back spring..." continued the old stag beetle.

"But... But what if spring never comes back?" questioned Lu.

"Oh, don't you worry. Spring will return," he replied. "Just close your tired eyes and before you know it, it'll be warm and sunny! Who knows? Maybe you'll even miss the snow!"

"I didn't even think about trying to find a place to sleep for the winter," said Lu in a small voice.

"Luckily, you have friends, Lu," said the orange-shelled ladybug. "In the fall, most of us were looking for the best hollow to hibernate. But let's be quick; the other ladybugs are waiting for us!"

Lu turned to the old stag beetle.

"Thank you, Mr. Stag Beetle. You sure know a lot about winter!"

"It was my pleasure! Old Beetle is always here to help! And now hurry along, my friends!" he said as he disappeared into the hollow of the tree.

Not wasting a minute, Lu and her friend flew over the snow-covered hills to dream their ladybug dreams in their new winter home. Lu snuggled into a bed of dry leaves and slept for a long, long time.

But what was happening outside?

More and more white snow fell on the ground as snow-storms came and went.

Whoooooosh!

Many animals and insects slept in their homes, except for a little gray mouse. He'd run out of food and decided to go looking for more in the snow....

After weeks and months of cold days and nights, the weather began to turn warmer and warmer. The snow slowly melted, making small streams and puddles on the ground. Winter was coming to an end.

One early morning, the little ladybug opened her eyes and yawned a big yawn.

"Has winter ended?" asked Lu.

"Yes, it has! Spring is here!" smiled the orange-shelled ladybug.

"Ah, my dear friends! Thank you for all your help!" Lu said. She smiled a bright smile and flew away to meet the new spring.

Lu saw that birds had returned to greet the warm weather.

The trees turned green and were waiting for their flowers to bloom.

The little ladybug twirled and whirled in the air, enjoying the warm wind on her wings.

Soon Lu found a new daisy for her new home. There, sitting on the white petals, she watched the many spring sunrises and sunsets.

Lu learned to be thankful for what she had; she knew that things might change, just like summers, falls, winters, and springs are changing all the time, again and again. But Lu knew she was not alone; she had plenty of trustworthy friends!

This is the story of a ladybug named Lu, who loved to fly and explore this beautiful world and felt ready to face any change with her newfound courage.

About the Author

Yuliya received a degree in economics in Ukraine and in education management in the US. She worked in a non-governmental sector for six years as a founder of the educational organisation for teacher's professional development in Ukraine. Yuliya is a mother of three boys who are the inspiration behind her stories. Her sons give her lots of ideas for engaging and meaningful stories every day. They are the first to read her stories and give her helpful feedback. Yuliya loves to share her writing and her journey through motherhood on her social media platforms. She loves spending time outdoors and with her family.

www.thewayswegrow.com

Follow the Author on Instagram
@the.ways.we.grow

Join on Twitter @AuthorYuliya

Read Two More Stories About Lu

If you enjoyed the Ladybug Lu Story leave your feedback on Amazon

CPSIA information can be obtained
at www.ICGtesting.com
Printed in the USA
LVHW071934141121
703304LV00002B/8